good deed rain

53 Books by Allen Frost

...Ohio Trio...Bowl of Water...Another Life...
...Home Recordings...The Mermaid Translation...
...The Selected Correspondence of Kenneth
Patchen...The Wonderful Stupid Man...
...Saint Lemonade...Playground...Roosevelt...
...5 Novels...The Sylvan Moore Show...
...Town in a Cloud...A Flutter of Birds Passing
Through Heaven: A Tribute to Robert Sund...
..At the Edge of America..Lake Erie Submarine..
...The Book of Ticks...I Can Only Imagine...
...The Orphanage of Abandoned Teenagers...
..Different Planet..Go With the Flow: A Tribute
to Clyde Sanborn...Homeless Sutra...
..The Lake Walker..A Hundred Dreams Ago..
..Almost Animals..The Robotic Age..Kennedy..
...Fable...Elbows & Knees: Essays and Plays...
...The Last Paper Stars...Walt Amherst is Awake...
....When You Smile You Let in Light....
...Pinocchio in America...Florida...
..Blue Anthem Wailing..The Welfare Office..
...Island Air...Imaginary Someone...
....Violet of the Silent Movies....
...The Tin Can Telephone...Heaven Crayon...
..Old Salt..A Field of Cabbages..River Road..
...The Puttering Marvel...Something Bright...
...The Trillium Witch...Cosmonaut...
...Thriftstore Madonna...Half a Giraffe...
..Lexington Brown & The Pond Projector..
.....The Robert Huck Museum.....
...Mrs. Magnusson & Friends...

Mrs. Magnusson & Friends

The blessed sunshine and the quiet moonlight shall come through our window.

—Nathaniel Hawthorne, "The Great Carbuncle"

MRS. MAGNUSSON
& FRIENDS

Allen Frost

Good Deed Rain ◊ Bellingham, Washington ◊ 2022

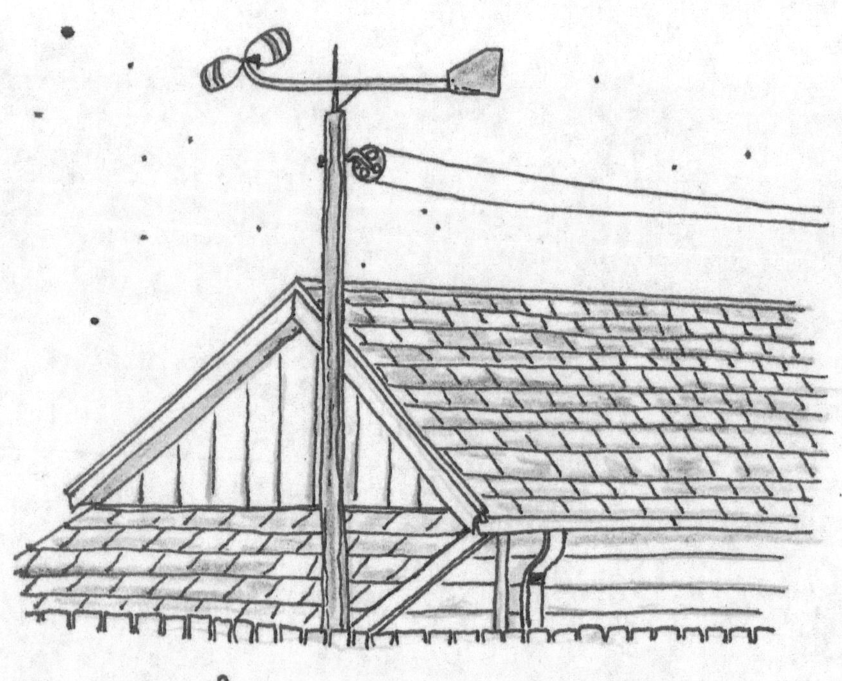

universal thirteen

INTRODUCTION

Who knows why these thirteen stories arrived? I just let them in the door. At the time, around Halloween, I had recently finished a novel, I was writing a little book of poems, I expected to write more, when this flew into our house like a pelican.

I'm reminded of two other little rare handsewn books I made long ago, *The Shrinkers* (1990) and *Universal Thirteen* (1999). This book is following their noble tradition, a collection of strange stories, familiar ground. In fact, one of the unpublished stories from *The Shrinkers* has been transformed as "Animals of the Moon." Three other stories from that old collection were printed in *The Sylvan Moore Show* (2015). So it's fitting that a new Sylvan Moore story would appear in these pages. You might also recognize some other stars of Good Deed Rain turning up throughout.

The Shrinkers (cover art by Robert Millis, c.1988)

Finally, Mrs. Magnusson is not fiction. She's someone J.Genius told me about, a teacher he never forgot. Her memory reappeared to him one day out of the blue and when he told me about her, I caught the fever too. She's the sort of one-in-a-million person that weaves their way into your life. Then he told me he tracked her down. And believe it or not, she lives just down the street from us! I walked the dog past her house. It's built right next to a power station. I can imagine her radiating in that glow. We saw the old VW van parked in her driveway. I don't want to give too much away, she was an inspiration, something fictional and wondrous, even if she's real.

—AF, November 13, 2021

CONTENTS

The NEXT ICHABOD CRANE.........................13

CUPID SHOOTS KID with ARROW................17

ALAMEDA SHOPPER'S GAZETTE...............23

ANIMALS of the MOON.........................29

CALLING HEAVEN.................................35

HOW the CIVIL WAR DOES LINGER............41

The FRIENDLY SORT................................45

MRS. MAGNUSSON.................................51

SEA WITCH...55

MURDER BY 78.....................................61

The BACKWARDS MAN............................65

The SONGWRITER.................................71

I MET SYLVAN MOORE...........................77

11

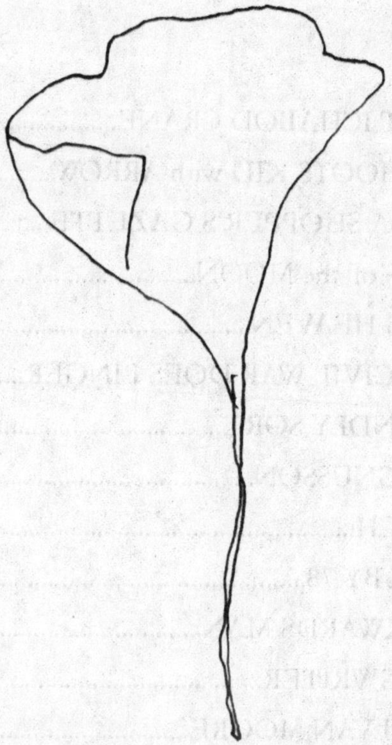

The NEXT ICHABOD CRANE

Of course I don't believe in The Headless Horseman. I live here in Sleepy Hollow where it happened, but I don't have to believe it. It's just a legend. A fairytale. Do you believe in The Three Bears? You have to draw the line somewhere. I don't let it bother me.

My name is Ichabod Crane. You think that's an easy name to live up to? I've been kidded since I was a kid. Now I don't mind. I got used to it. It rolls off me like water.

"Ichabod! Do I pay you to daydream?"

"No, sir," I jumped. "I'm sorry."

My boss halted next to my desk. "Did you get that report done?"

I'm an idiot. I let it slip my mind. "Almost…" I spread some papers around. How could I forget about it?

"You're not leaving until you do."

"Yes, I won't."

He tapped his watch, "It's already five, Crane. You'll work here all night if you have to." He pointed at his office behind the glass wall, "I want to see it on my desk when I get here tomorrow."

I nodded, "You have my word." People of the future won't believe what we put up with. I guarantee that.

He was still steaming as he left, but I was busy opening drawers, trying to find that report. No wonder I forgot about it. It was buried under an inch of paper. "The Annual

Proficiency Report to Annuity Shareholders." There's a title you won't find on the bestseller list. No wonder I hid it from view. Subconsciously of course.

A bank of lights along the back wall went out. I looked up and waved at Janet over by the door. "I'm still here!" I called.

"It's five, Ichabod!"

"I know. I have to finish this darn report."

She said, "Ugh," and waved, "Good luck!"

I heard the door click and then I was the only one in the office. I had to make charts. I had to crunch numbers and write conclusions. It took me hours. The daylight was long gone. When I finally put the report on my boss' desk and left the office, turned off the switches by the door, I was in the black. It's a good thing I know my way outside, after all the time I've spent here I could do it blindfolded.

An eerie green light gloomed on the sidewalk. My bike was where I left it this morning, chained to a broomstick tree. They kid me about riding a bike to work, but like I said, teasing doesn't bother me.

Sleepy Hollow is a modern town, at least this part of town, but it's pretty desolate in the evenings. Industrial zoning, big lots fenced with barbed wire, warehouses. When the road skirted the edge of a neighborhood, I could see lights in the windows of the houses. Everyone's home after a long day, watching *The Honeymooners*, or *Route 66*. They were all in for the night. I steered past their parked cars, Oldsmobiles, Plymouths, station wagons, and Mercuries.

The road curved towards the river. I live on the other side of the bridge. Of course everyone knows the story of the bridge, how someone named Ichabod Crane would have been free if only he could have crossed that bridge. So far, I've crossed it all my life just fine. I don't believe in fairytales; it doesn't worry me. I see the lights of the depot over there. The sky to the south is orange from the oil refinery over on March Point. I remember when I was a kid, they used to say witches would fly on nights like these.

The bridge came into view around a big shadowy heap of slag. A car banged across the plates headed this way. And that's when my bike hit something on the road. The handlebars jerked out of my hands and I was lucky I caught the grips and steadied myself on the gravel. My hands were shaking. There was enough light from the sodium streetlamps to see what I ran over. How ridiculous...

I leaned the bike on its kickstand and kneeled by the front wheel. A horseshoe was pinned to the flat tire. One of those rusty nails did the trick. I don't question things like this, I'm not surprised—there's a formula for the near impossible. Math explains everything. That's an accountant for you.

I wrenched the horseshoe off, tossed it against a fence, where it wouldn't likely find another bicycle tire. Does history repeat? Can time wind itself round and round? Maybe every hundred years another Ichabod Crane comes along. I hope the next one does better.

This Ichabod Crane was doomed to push a bike with a flat tire. I know fairytales aren't supposed to end like this, but like I said at the beginning, I don't believe in them.

CUPID SHOOTS KID with ARROW

She read the teletype, "Cupid shoots kid with arrow, truck drives off dock, Japan bombs Pearl Harbor."

"Wait a minute!" he interrupted. "What did you say?"

"Japan bombs Pearl Harbor."

"Before that."

"Truck drives off dock?"

"No…Further back."

"Cupid shoots kid with arrow."

"Yeah…That's the one I like."

Margie rolled her eyes.

He nodded, "Yes, I want you to follow up on that."

"Oh, brother. What about the truck? What happened to the driver, was it carrying top secrets, is it still underwater?"

"Forget the truck, Margie. You do this Cupid story for us and you can have your pick of the next one."

"Really?" She whistled. "You must feel awful strongly about it."

"I do." He was serious. He resembled the photo of F.D.R. on the wall behind him.

So she agreed. It would be fine. It was the sort of story that wrote itself. She could get all the details she needed in one visit to Dayton Street. She wrote the address on a pad in her purse and was on her way.

The car radio stations were all about Pearl Harbor. Margie kept turning the dial. It was hard to find something by Lady Day and Prez. It wasn't a long drive. The back streets of town were calm. Finally, she turned the radio off and steered with both hands. "Cupid…" she said. She thought of the boy, the victim, and stopped herself—she didn't want preconceptions, she wanted to walk into their house with an open mind.

723 Dayton was a piece of work. Charlie Chaplin could come walking out the door, tip on the slanted porch, trip down the funhouse stairs and roll like an acrobat up to the bare pear tree.

She walked carefully on the path, around a mushed pear muzzled by bees. It seemed late for pears, late for bees too. This was a yard where things lingered.

The Chaplin stairs creaked beneath her. The creaks continued across the porch like her shadow. Margie looked in the window and across the room she saw a deer head mounted on the wall. A red shotgun shell leaned on the windowsill. This house was no stranger to hunting. No, she warned her imagination, don't jump to conclusions. The deer stared at her. It was a great detail for her story.

She knocked on the door.

A woman wearing a housedress crossed the room and opened the door. "Yes?"

"Hello, my name is Margie Hendricks, I'm from the *Herald*. Do you have a moment?"

"Is this about Billy?"

Margie smiled, "Well, yes actually. How is he?"

"Oh, he'll be fine. He's got his leg all bandaged up."

"You see, we heard he was shot by an arrow and the editor thought there's a story you don't hear every day! I'm sure our readers would be interested if you're willing to share. A slow day like this and your news ought to make front page."

"Oh, that's fine! This will cheer him up!" Billy's mother invited Margie inside. "Right this way," she said. Before she opened the door, she lowered her voice, "Billy thinks it was some flying angel that shot him. Cupid." She shut her eyes. "Maybe you can get the truth out of him."

Margie saluted. "I'll do my best."

Billy's mother tapped the door, "Honey? It's me. I've got a newspaper reporter here who'd like to speak with you. That okay, honey?"

Billy sighed and said, "Okay…"

The door swung open and Margie observed a room that looked like it had been wrestled to the ground. "Oh, Billy!" his mother cried. "Look at this mess!" She turned swiftly to her visitor and held Margie's arm, "Don't write about this, okay?"

Margie consoled her, "Oh don't worry, Billy's the star of the story. How are you, Billy?"

The boy laying in a crumpled bed reading *Popular Mechanics* sat up. "I'm fine. I told the police what happened but they didn't believe me."

"What did happen, Billy?" Margie asked.

"They thought I shot myself, but I didn't. It was Cupid that did it."

"Cupid? The little round baby with wings?"

"That's the guy. And now I know why. Will you go to the movies with me?

"What?"

"The picture at the Avalon. Barbara Stanwyck is in it." He rested his magazine on his leg and winced, "You know what? You kind of look like her."

"Wait a minute, slow down. Tell me more about this Cupid incident."

"I was out in the backyard. We have winter cabbage growing. I was checking on them like I always do and I heard something buzzing loud in the air. I thought it was maybe one of those new autogyros I was reading about. But it was Cupid. Just like you'd imagine him to be. The messenger of love." He rubbed his leg. "Now that you're here, I feel better. What's your name? I'm sure it's something lovely."

"Oh brother, you are a wolf."

"A wounded wolf," he pouted.

Billy's mother crept beside Margie and presented her with the arrow that struck her son. It looked like a movie prop. One overall yellow color, harmless as a toy.

"Cupid shot this?"

"That's right. Then flew away. I had an arrow in my leg, Ma called the doctor. He bandaged me up. The police came, they talked to me and left. And now you're here and I'm in love."

"How old are you, Billy?"

"Eighteen. You can call me William if you want. There's a matinee in an hour. *Ball of Fire*, Barbara Stanwyck plays a dancehall dynamo who falls in love with a shy introvert, like me."

Margie laughed. "I gotta take a picture of this kid before I get heartburn," she quipped. She slung around the camera she wore and hoisted it to her eye. "Say cheese, Billy!" There was a loud pop of light, burned ozone, and she said, "Got it."

Billy's mother waved at the air with a shirt she picked off the floor.

Margie coughed. "Listen kid," she said, "Don't get me wrong—you're the most precocious, overconfident, spoiled young man I've ever met—but you'll be fine, don't worry. You're going to get better. You've got a sweetheart somewhere out there. Have a little faith. Just give it time, okay? One day she'll find you. You'll notice her and it'll hit you just like that dopey arrow."

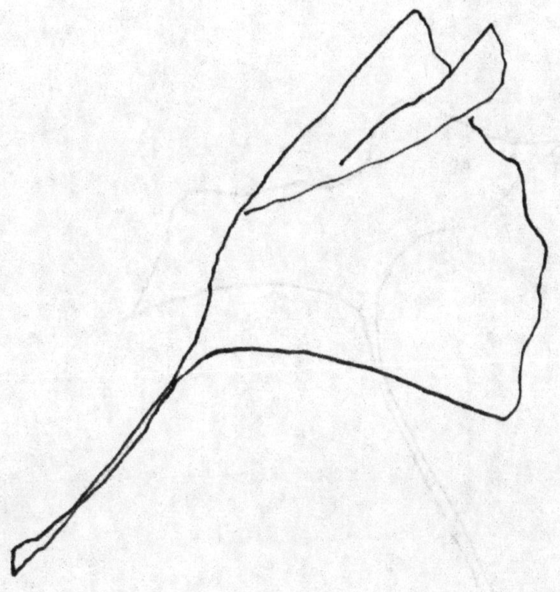

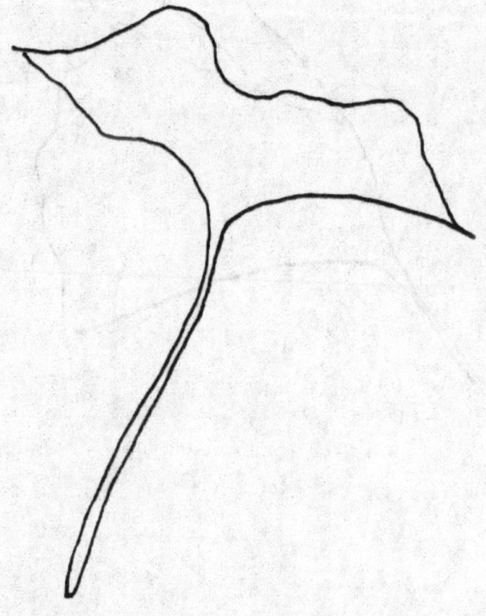

They were living in his car. They just needed a little cash, a job, any job, to get them started. When she found the listing in the *Alameda Shopper's Gazette*, she showed it to him. He figured why not? They could do that for the day, and she agreed.

The big palms of Neptune Park were holding a bright sun. They followed Central Avenue to the address of Lincoln Appliance Sales & Repair. Pete held Liesel's hand. "There it is," she said.

A yellow sign hung from the awning like a ginkgo leaf.

"Good luck," he said, squeezing her hand.

If it went okay, they would each get twenty-five dollars. That seemed pretty good for four hours of handing out flyers.

The shop was a little worn, the window was filled with TVs and vacuum cleaners and old radios. Inside was more of the same. Pete held the door open for Liesel. A layer of cigar smoke drew a line in the air. Liesel headed for the man at the counter who was watching *Sesame Street* of all things. He faced them and took the cigar from his mouth.

Once they told him they were interested in the job, his demeanor changed. "Hi kids, my name's Horton Booth." He asked about them and they told him they were new in Alameda and having a hard time, but they knew it would get better. He agreed and he complimented Liesel's green hair and he told them what a great job he had for them. He had two paper shopping bags packed with flyers for his store. "Alameda's a big town," he grinned.

Liesel said, "I was thinking we could hand out a lot at Safeway."

Horton shook his head, "Try to stay in motion."

"What, like dancing?" Liesel asked, twisting her hips.

"No, I mean like don't stay in one place too long. Keep moving. And if anybody asks, you don't know me."

Pete said, "Mister Booth, is this illegal?"

"No, of course not," he said. "I just think it's better for you to hit as many places as you can. You'll get the hang of it, you're a smart couple." He pushed the bags towards them.

Liesel lifted the handles of one. "Whew! How many are in here?"

"Enough to make a difference," he answered. "It's hard work for a place like this, going against Sears and Woolworths. A real Davey and Goliath situation."

With a loud crackling, Pete tucked his bag under his arm.

Horton didn't like something about that. "Whatever you do, don't throw them away, I have ways of knowing."

"We won't," Liesel promised.

"I know all the garbage cans of town. These flyers cost me a lot of dough. I hired you because you look honest to me. Don't prove me wrong."

"We won't, Mr. Booth," Liesel promised. Pete was tugging her sleeve.

Horton stood and spoke with his cigar glowing, "And don't come back before four o'clock."

Pete held the door for Liesel again and he waved as they left. A faint spool of cigar smoke followed him out and vanished in the sunlight.

Liesel was already handing a flyer to a woman pushing a baby carriage. "There's lots of great deals. You could use a foot massager. I saw one listed in here." The woman laughed and took the flyer and Liesel made a face at Pete when the carriage wheeled away.

"Nice job," he kissed her. It turned out she was a natural at the art of peddling. Pete discovered he wasn't. He could tell he would never make a living like this. Liesel had rapport and a natural friendliness, that's the way she was, she made it look easy. After an hour, he became the official flyer carrier and let her do all the talking. That worked much better.

They finished most of one bag. He poured them together in one bag, and they were in front of Safeway and Liesel was right about that spot, they were doing well, there was a lot of foot traffic. She could drop a flyer in each of the grocery bags going by. They thought they were doing fine until a police car arrived.

"Liesel…" Pete said. He had a feeling. When you live in a car on the street, that sense is honed as a skipping stone. "Liesel!" She was talking to someone about the weather when he squeezed her arm. "Liesel, we have to go." He saw the car door open as an officer got out and he seized her, "We have to go now!"

"What's the matter?"

"Come on!"

She dropped some flyers as they ran past the wide Safeway windows, around the corner of the pale-yellow building into a dead-end alley. Pete drew her in behind a big dumpster full of cardboard. "What's the matter?" Liesel repeated.

"The cops. You didn't see them. I don't think we're supposed to be doing this."

"Oh, Pete! They're not going to do anything to us. The worst they can do is tell us to leave."

"Maybe. I don't know. I don't like this job." And with that, he heaved the paper bag up over the edge of the dumpster.

"Pete! Mr. Booth will find it! He said so!"

"No he won't." And just so she wouldn't worry, he climbed the dumpster and reached in and pushed the bag beneath a broken apple box, covered it with more flattened crates and a copy of the *Alameda Shoppers Gazette*. It was sunk under waves of cardboard. He hopped back to the cement and was going to promise her everything was okay. They could wait until four o'clock. He could pull down some cardboard for them to sit on. They could do the crossword in the *Gazette*. Everything would be alright.

Liesel wasn't looking for that comfort though. She was staring out of the alley at the man who stood there, holding a smoldering cigar.

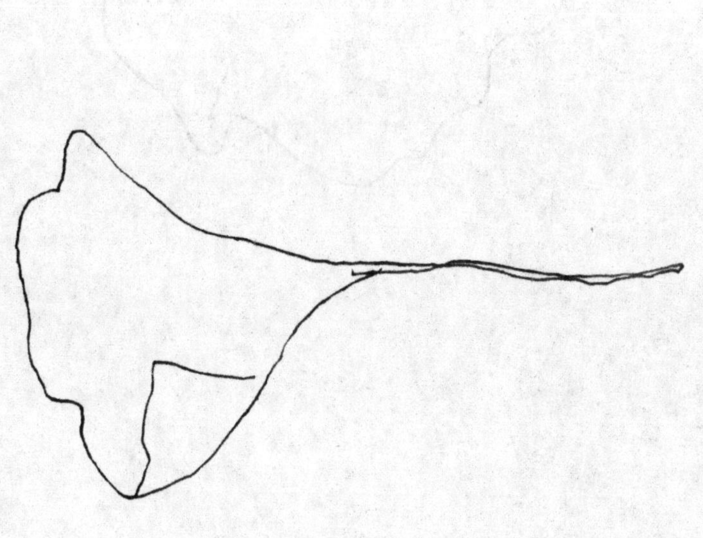

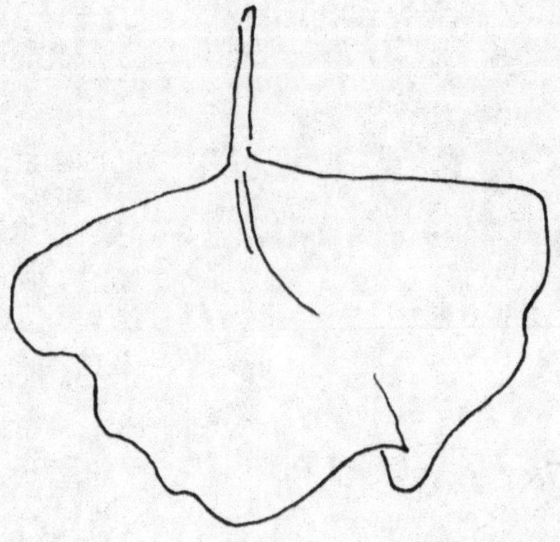

ANIMALS of the MOON

His friends laughed when he told them he had seen a mountain lion. "What? In your yard?" "Yeah, sure you did!" "Right next to the grizzly bear?" As if animals weren't meant to be believed. In the small space of his trailer, he sat watching one of those detective shows on TV, the kind where the private eye has an idea to solve the crime and even though no one will believe him, he sticks to his guns, follows his lead, and ends up trapped with a beautiful woman reporter in an alley, menaced by thugs in a black limo, until there is a commercial for used cars.

"No, I really did see a mountain lion," he told the telephone. "I heard it too. It was right outside my window." There was laughter on the other end of the line, but he knew what he saw. He looked at the dull black window that reflected the lightbulb hanging from the ceiling like a 75-watt sun. He couldn't see the night, but it was out there.

His dog put a paw on the door and whined.

"I have to go," he said. "Goldie wants out." He said goodbye and said yes, he would watch out for mountain lions, very funny, and then he hung up. Goldie stared over her shoulder at him. "Okay, okay," he said.

There was a moment when he opened the door just wide enough for him to look out, with Goldie pressed against the back of his legs, when he could see the yard lit by the trailer window and everything else was shadows and tall trees and the gunmetal shards of the cloudy sky. In this day and age, with the highway cutting through the slope of woods and houses and streets and convenience stores, it didn't seem like a mountain lion's world anymore. He didn't mean to let her out yet, he only wanted to make sure the coast was clear. "Alright, Goldie." He moved a leg and she leaped from the trailer.

"Hey! Easy!" He clapped his hands, "Goldie!" but the dog was already gone, running into the brush. He sighed as he left the doorway to slip his shoes on. He wasn't going after Goldie in bare feet. He grabbed his coat too. The TV continued. Three mafia-types with sunglasses stepped out of the limousine and walked towards the detective and the reporter, looming in the headlights.

Zipping his coat, he shut the door and stepped to the ground. No moon. The night was just as black last night when he heard the mountain lion. He called for Goldie and listened… nothing. He left the pool of trailer light and crunched to the edge of the gravelly dirt driveway where a gutted stone fence marked the beginning of a long stretch of wild blue field leading into the black woods in the distance. The two of them knew this landscape by day, at night Goldie could be hiding in it anywhere. There were other animals in it too, any rabbit or deer could have caught her attention. He listened for the sounds of her.

Far off to the right he could hear the riverlike rush of the interstate. That dull sigh was steady all the time. To his left, across the field a few lights shined in the shapes of a house. Somewhere in between was Goldie.

"Goldie!" He picked up a stone and threw it. Silent in the air, it ricocheted with a loud click off another glacial rock. The loud crack echoed down the field, off the faraway forest and back.

Around a tree, he stepped cautiously into the field, into the sighing wild grass bent in the cool breeze. A wandering owl sailed against the clouds hunting mice. What would he do if the lion was waiting for him? He grabbed a branch big enough to be a club. It was better than nothing. He smelled the air, imagining through the earthy scent of pine and cedar, searching for the dark rush, looking for the glowing yellow eyes and listening. Goldie got him moving again, he couldn't leave her out here alone.

He was a hundred feet into the brush and his eyes were getting used to the dark. When the moon emerged from the clouds it was like a spotlight on the animal draped over a log. "Oh no!" he cried and ran to it.

Down on the ground, shredded in half, torn to pieces, the head was ripped from the shoulders, with stuffing scattered around, one arm standing in the air waving for help. He kicked at the sewn together pink toy, the white fluff came out and drifted like feathers over the weeds. It was the Pink Panther, from that cartoon, a big one, about four feet tall when it was whole. A fairground prize someone won in one of those gaming booths.

He was scaring himself.

He started through the field again, almost tripping on an unseen blackberry vine.

In the summertime the faint sounds of the fair carried in the air, wheezing and breathing, but they had been gone for months, packed up and left like the geese flying south. Another cloud covered the moon.

He called for his dog again. Where was she? Did she go this far?

Only the racket of his legs sawing through the tall grass and brambles, breathing hard. That torn up panther got to him. Why feel like he was next?

He ran and ran over the stumbling ground, and didn't stop until he reached a tree at the edge of the forest. He put his arm against the rough bark, exhausted and panting. Swallowing, trying to get his breath back.

There was a sound in the woods, snapping twigs.

He was too tired, if it was the mountain lion then it was meant to be.

What a surprise to have Goldie run up to him instead. She whined and jumped against him, spinning around his legs, wagging her tail, whap, whap, whap. He ran his hands through her silky fur and laughed with relief. Held tightly in her mouth was a crushed leprechaun.

"What do you have?" he asked. "Let me see that."

She didn't want to let it go. But as he kneeled down he could feel it was another fairground toy, a felt mouse dressed like a leprechaun, top hat, belt buckle, and satin suit. "What is this? Where'd you get this?"

Goldie bounded away from him and he followed that wagging tail. He wished he would've brought her leash. She was free and loving this cool night. Once he caught up with her again, he would have to grab her and lead her home by the collar. She looked back at him from a fern, still holding that leprechaun.

He broke through more blackberries and scratches as she took him over a hill. The clouds parted and ahead of them the hillside was lined with moonlit silhouettes like an audience. He stopped running and froze. Stuffed animal prizes surrounded them. A hundred of them. As the season ended, someone at the fair shucked them in the woods like a balloon leaving ballast behind. All the prizes were dumped or tossed out into the brush. Or maybe someone won them and left them around as a gag. The tall arches of trees and the glow of the moon made a cathedral, every animal quiet and calm, until one of them moved.

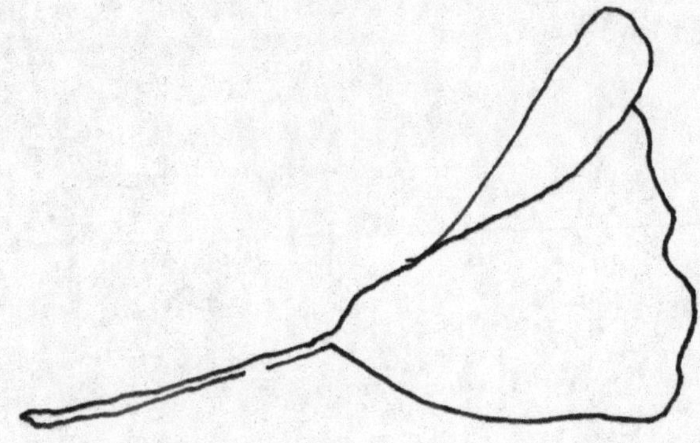

CALLING HEAVEN

You can't just call Heaven on an ordinary phone. At the moment it happens to be a phonebooth on the corner of Elwood Avenue. Planted like a yucca next to the road. Not a popular spot. A steep hill climbs from it, up to the apartments. There's not even a crosswalk. You have to want to use that payphone. Someone always does. He wanted to talk to Heaven.

How did a two-bit crook like Gerald Neffley get a chance to talk to the dearly departed, when all around him people came and went without a clue? He had connections. He had his ear to the ground. People like him usually do. Someone who knew someone who knew someone told him it was there. It was one of those magical things that appear and disappear like a rainbow, he knew he had to act while he could.

The phonebooth didn't look like it served such a glorious purpose. A window was cracked. The metal was scratched and with the door bent, it wouldn't close all the way. He brought the receiver to his ear and dropped some coins in the slot and waited.

"One moment please," the operator told him.

Put on hold. He listened to a harpsichord version of the Doors. He heard the whole thing. There was a pause then a Beatles song began. Was this a telephone or a jukebox?

A click. The operator returned to remind him, "Please deposit another twenty-five cents."

Gerald checked his pockets, one after the other. "Listen, I

don't have it. Can you please give me a little more time? Just a minute. I need to talk to my brother, tell him everything's okay. I'll do whatever you want when you get me there. I promise. I'll dust harps, sweep clouds, whatever."

The operator thought it over.

She pressed a button.

A cement-mixer truck smashed over the phonebooth.

Gerald appeared before her.

"Okay," she told him, "Welcome to Heaven. I'm going on break. You can sit on this chair until I get back."

He called after her, "What am I supposed to do?"

She shrugged off the question and got lost in a cloud.

"Hello?"

Gerald turned around.

A girl stared at him.

"Hello…" he said and remembered what he heard, "Welcome to Heaven."

"This is Heaven?" She didn't seem impressed. They were surrounded by thick clouds that shifted and swerved.

"Yes…Apparently…" He sat down. There was a spindly table stand with just enough room for a phone on it. He wasn't sure what he was supposed to say. He only arrived a moment before her. "Sorry, there's not much to see, it's a little cloudy today."

The girl shrugged.

He clasped his hands together. Where was that angel operator he was talking to? She didn't explain anything.

"Do you let me in?" the girl asked him.

What was he supposed to say? "Yes. Of course, right this way." He swept his arm, noticing for the first time that he was wearing a long robe. That made sense, being Heaven and all. He liked the way it flowed.

She went past him and already there was someone else standing where she had been.

An old man grinned at Gerald.

"Oh, go ahead," Gerald said. He wanted a chance to look around, but there was already another person popped into place.

He let quite a few go by. They kept appearing.

He just waved them through. It seemed never-ending as a waterfall.

If they came all this way, shouldn't they be let in?

That's what he figured.

They walked by into the bank of clouds behind him. He hoped there was plenty of room back there.

The telephone rang. He let another person into Heaven then he answered the phone as he assumed he was meant to, "Welcome to Heaven," he said.

"Gerry? Is that you?"

"Muldoon?"

"Hey, Neff. I was sorry to hear about you."

"Are you calling from that phonebooth?"

"Yeah, only it's not in the same place. That cement mixer really did a job on it. But at least it was quick, right? I bet you didn't know what hit you."

Gerald placed his hand over the receiver and said, "Welcome to Heaven," to the next starry-eyed citizen. Then he returned to the conversation, "What do you want, Muldoon?"

"What do I *want?*" Muldoon choked. "Out of the goodness of my heart, I call you in Heaven to see how my old friend is doing. I shed tears for you, Gerry and look how you treat me."

"Please deposit another twenty-five cents," Gerald said.

"Gerry!"

"What do you want, Muldoon. I'm busy."

"Okay, I'll tell you. I need money. Just tell me where you got that stash hidden. It won't do you any good now."

Gerald laughed. He couldn't help it. He didn't care about money—that America was a million miles away. It had no hold on him anymore.

"Gerry! You listening? Come on Gerry, what can I do for you in return? You got any loose ends?"

Gerald meant to hang up. Someone was patiently waiting to get into Heaven. All he had to do was put the receiver back in its cradle, and it looked like he was doing just that, but as he began to, something devilish lingered in his smile. He pressed the red button beside the rotary dial.

A phonebooth, the same one that sent Gerald to Heaven, the same one that kept reappearing in vacant lots and dead ends, blew up. A broken gas line. These things happen. And Muldoon was standing on a cloud.

"Welcome to Heaven," said Gerald. The job was no mystery anymore, he had been here long enough to know what to do, "I'm going on break," he told Muldoon, "You can sit on this chair until I get back."

"Wait! Gerry! You can't leave, you can't leave me here. Where am I, what do I do?"

Muldoon's voice faded out with every step away. Gerald walked into the nearest soft wall of cloud and then he was through. No wonder people were in such a rush to get here.

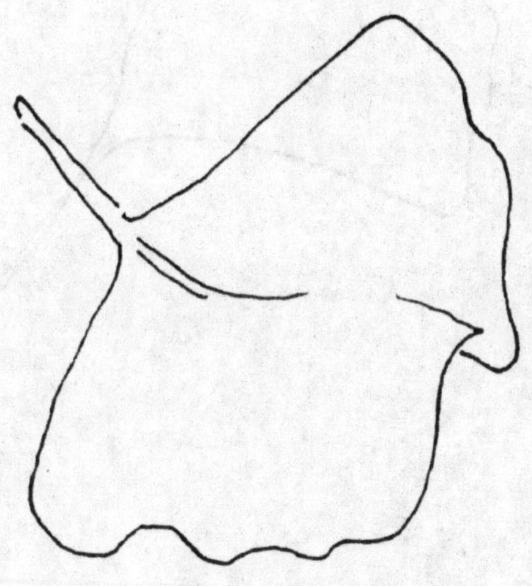

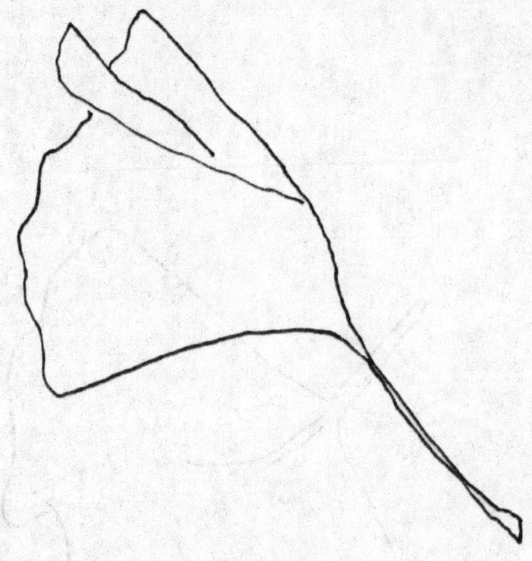

HOW the CIVIL WAR DOES LINGER

Outside the Winn-Dixie, two Confederate soldiers approached a parked car. One of them kept a hand on his saber. Even if this parking lot wasn't officially a battlefield, you couldn't be too careful. It was a sunny day, the cars sparkled chrome, an ambush was in order.

Sitting behind the wheel, a Union infantryman was eating a sandwich and reading a paperback book. A bit of egg salad stuck to his moustache. His blue cap rested on the dashboard. His windows were rolled down, he was an easy target—he could have been reading Walt Whitman in the middle of a field, his horse cropping daisies beneath him. Orioles whistling in the trees. He didn't notice them until a musket barrel swung across the page. He looked up from his book, "Well, hello there. Harry, Toby. How are you fellows doing?"

Harry laughed. "You're a dead man, Yates!"

Yates waved his sandwich, "Okay, you got me."

They stood by the car door and grinned, two musty gray Colonel uniforms. Then Toby asked, "You eating lunch?" He always had an eye for a meal. That missing gold button that popped off his uniform was a casualty of that appetite.

Yates nodded, "I couldn't wait for the siege. I got this at the deli and—Oh!" He turned his shoulder, one stripe sewn on, "I brought ice-coffee. Thirsty?"

They were of course, and like any other soldier prepared for the day's fighting, they carried tin cups with their kit.

A little hospitality was all that was needed. Maybe the horror of Gettysburg could have been averted like this. Yates poured each officer a full cup and raised his own in a toast.

Harry had a loud, satisfied sip. But his hungry Confederate comrade became a casualty. It happened in a split second. Toby gave a shriek and dumped a black stain down the front of his uniform. His tin cup clacked on the tar and a bee flew off the splash. Harry took a swing at it with his sword, too late. Toby flailed his hand.

"It get you?"

"I don't know, I don't know," Toby balled his hand and wailed, "Hurts…I think so. I think it bit me."

"And look at your uniform," Harry said. "What a mess."

"I know, I can't show up for war like this. Already dead…" In black and white film, the spill would read as blood.

Yates had some paper napkins he passed out the window, but they didn't help much. Then he offered, "You know, I might have something else for you," and he opened the car door. "Come on back," he said as they shuffled out of his way. "I got something you can borrow."

He popped the trunk. There was a cardboard box, a saber, a folded dry cleaner bag he lifted by the hanger. Yates unzipped it and withdrew the suit, "This here is an exact replica of Sergeant William Harvey Carney's uniform, 54th Massachusetts Volunteer Infantry, including as you can see his Medal of Honor."

"That's nice," Toby nodded. He clutched his wounded hand.

"You can't wear that!" Harry blustered.

Yates shrugged. "What difference does it make? We're all the same, we all think we're in the right. You can pretend you have a family back in New England. They're waiting for you to

42

come home when it's all over."

"What about me?" Harry barked, "We can't fight alongside each other!"

"No, I imagine not," Yates said, "Not this time."

Toby took the hanger handle with his good hand. "I like it," he decided. "Thanks."

Yates gave a little bow, "My pleasure."

"So that's it?" Harry looked troubled. Suddenly he was alone on the battlefield.

"I'll go in the store and put it on." Toby started on his way to Winn-Dixie, across the hot parking lot. Half a mile away, the municipal field was filling with soldiers. Tents, kitchens, flags, pickups, cars and buses. A row of vintage cannons was lining up on the lawn.

"Hey Toby!" Harry stopped him. He took a breath and his voice hitched, "Get some salve for that hand."

His friend's hand was still bunched in a pained fist. "I will." He saluted.

"Baking soda would be better," Yates advised.

Harry bit his lip and glared at the red and white grocery sign posted high above the cars. Some buzzards pivoted against the sky. A thermal kept them pinned up there.

The FRIENDLY SORT

I'm friendly to a fault. Nobody's perfect, personalities and quirks follow us around, but my flaw led me here, to prison. You wouldn't think being friendly would cause this, but so it goes. People are a little surprised how gullible I am. I can't help it.

Still, it was my fault I got talked into robbing a bank.

"What can you tell us about them?"

"I don't know. They were wearing masks." Everyone wore masks nowadays, it was a boon time for robberies, I'm sure.

"Anything at all, Mr. Klerk?"

"No…Honestly, they were just a couple of guys wearing masks. They needed my help." One thing led to another. The next thing I knew I was standing in the alley next to the bank, tossing a canvas bag through an open window of a getaway car that roared and bounced through puddles and screeched onto Chestnut Street while the alarm bell rang.

The policeman sighed. "Anything you remember about their car?"

I rubbed my forehead. I wished I could help.

I think they put me in jail as an example. They needed to lock someone behind bars. They want the world to know that crime doesn't pay. I complied.

My cell is a place to think, to stare at the wall and see pictures in it of where I went wrong.

The chipped paint becomes Charlie's Quality Cars. Charlie

pulled me off the sidewalk and next thing I know I was standing beside a heaped over Chevrolet. It looked like it was praying for me. I told him I wasn't in the market for a car, but he insisted this car wouldn't be around much longer, he already had a customer, but he wanted me to have it. "Are you saying you don't think you deserve such a fine car?" Charlie said in disbelief. "Don't pass it up. Do yourself a favor. Buy this car or by the time you get back it will be gone."

The next scratch on the wall was that Vega I bought, when it broke down three blocks from Charlie's. That's what set me out walking. That's how I ended up at the next paint abstraction, Columbia Bank and my part in the robbery.

How did that happen anyway? My eyes slid along the wall. There I was, catching the bag falling out the window, just like they asked me to do.

I have plenty of time to stare at the wall. I can follow it around the narrow room like a movie. Can you believe it? I was only there a month and I was already seeing things. That wasn't good...

Maybe the warden took pity on me. Is that possible? I don't know how these things work, but somehow I got sent out with a work crew. That's a pretty good gig in jail. For once you're not surrounded by walls and barbed wire. I was almost free.

There's about ten of us, we go down the street weeding along the sidewalk, also picking up whatever trash we find. We drag bags along with us as we go. We got further from the County Corrections bus. I know we were all feeling it, but it wouldn't do to run. Just be glad to be outside, this close to an America we only dreamed of.

Across the street, I saw a car pull into a driveway and a woman got out and looked at us. She got her groceries and hurried inside her house. I imagine she locked the door. I returned to edging the sidewalk. We all had little shovels. Mine struck something pushed deeply into the knotted fallen leaves.

My first thought was, "What if it's a gun?" What a crazy thing to think. I reached down to feel what made that metallic clink. Not that I'd want a gun or know what to do with one. If it was one, I'm sure I'd give it to the guard if he asked for it.

I brushed the weeds and leaves off. It was an odd smooth shape. I laughed. It looked like one of those oil lamps a genie lives inside. One by one everyone in the crew took notice of me as I stood up with the lamp.

Clark hissed at me, "Go on! Wake up the genie!" Laughter cackled down the line.

I nodded and rubbed the corroded surface.

And just like that, a genie appeared. Not much of a genie. He looked like he spent his time tramping from town to town. He held out his ragged sleeves and bowed slightly and grated, "Your wish is my command."

I was too surprised to do anything, but the other inmates were yelling at me, "Make a wish! Get us out of here! Hurry!"

All that commotion was too much for the guard though. Haskins bounded over, "Gimme that!"

I did. With the lamp in new hands, the genie shuffled over the sidewalk to stand beside the guard and he repeated, "Your wish is my command."

I couldn't believe the way the other inmates reacted to me. I felt awful that I let them down. I had no idea.

The guard was happy. He held the lamp in both hands and told the genie what he wanted.

There was a loud pop and we all jumped.

Beside the curb a black car rumbled.

"Now I want a million dollars in the trunk," the guard said.

The Dodge Challenger's trunk flipped open and we could

all see the stacks of money.

"Give me ten million," the guard said.

With another snap in the air, more money appeared.

Haskins guffawed. "On second thought, just fill the trunk."

"You've had your three wishes," the genie told him.

"Fine," he grinned and dropped the lamp. "I'm good with that." His rosy face beamed. "I'm plenty good." He waddled quickly to the trunk and shut it, then he went around the shiny siding to the driver's door and got in. He was done with us. With a roar, the car peeled out onto the street, his arm out the window, one finger held up to salute his abandoned work crew.

It didn't take them long. Clark and the rest were over the lawn headed to the woods beyond. That seemed crazy to me. I stood there. Honestly, I wasn't sure what to do.

The genie reached in his coat pocket and got a cigarette. He offered me one and I smiled and took it to be neighborly, I guess. I don't smoke. I looked down the street. Our bus was still parked there. The driver was probably taking a nap.

The lamp sat on the sidewalk beside us. I picked it up and passed it to him. I asked, "Do you have to go back in there?"

He shook his head, "Not yet." He tucked the lamp under his arm and we stood there while he smoked his cigarette. He was deep in thought. I don't know what a genie got out of it, he looked pretty tired to me.

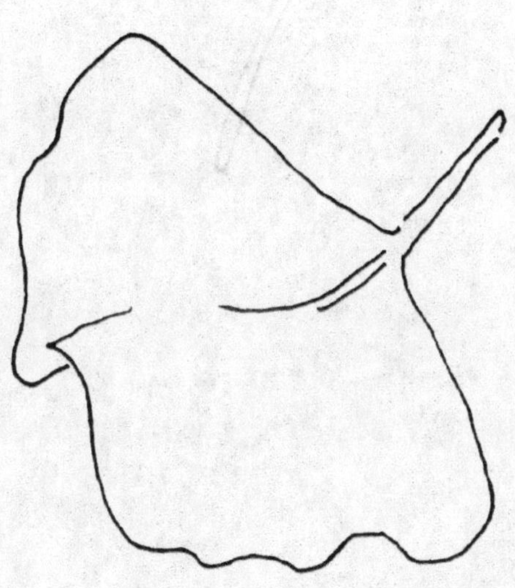

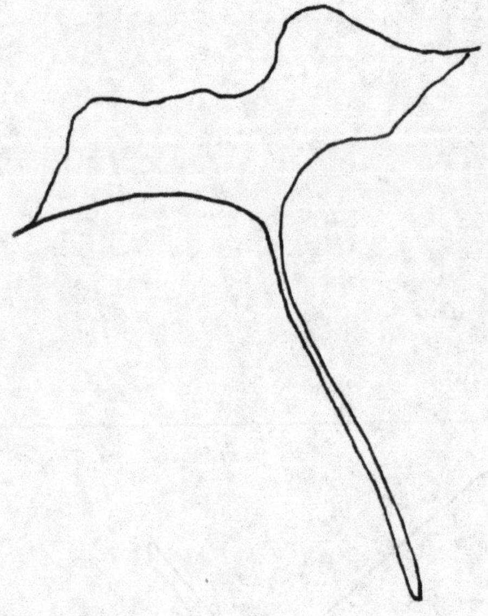

MRS. MAGNUSSON

All of a sudden, he thought of her. Forty years disappeared. He was in 5th grade and she was a volunteer who came to his class. Mrs. Magnusson wanted to be a teacher, he guessed. But he didn't see how that would happen. She didn't seem the type. She had a limp like a sailor when she walked your way. Maybe it was the thick waffle-sole shoes. He remembered her perfectly, the dusky coat she wore, her orange plaid pants, her copper hair balled on her head with yarn. She wore coke bottle glasses that turned her eyes into milky swirls. After a while, one eyeball would slide out of rhythm and it never failed, if she asked the class a question, she would look at one kid and point at another. Then there was her mouth. Her teeth were held in place by twisted wire braces. A brutal medieval-looking meshwork. There were places where the wiring was bent and stuck out like barbed wire. She ducked an imaginary bird and leaned and she liked to get right in close when she asked her question.

Caspar was ten. He wore a blue velour V-neck shirt with a chocolate milk stain. When she zeroed in on him, he couldn't move. He stared into those weird eyes, the left one wiggling a little, her mouth close enough to count each stitch of jagged tin. "Sorry…what did you say, Mrs. Magnusson?"

"Oh Caspar…" she stood up and coiled her hand around her green scarf. "You must learn to listen. We all must…" she cupped her hand to her ear and swiveled. "That's the only way you'll ever hear the crickets." Then she tapped the book she held, "Did you bring your book, Caspar?"

"No, I forgot."

"That's alright," she said, "You can borrow mine," and she passed it to him. "Can you please turn to page forty-two?"

He opened the book and in a few loud flips he found the page.

"Now, I want you to turn your book upside down."

He remembered laughing. He remembered the words falling off the page onto his desk. Little tumbles and tracks of black ink. He could rub the letters like coaldust between his fingertips.

Did that really happen?

Caspar stopped and stared at the gray sky. It was an ordinary rainy day. He was walking home from work. Why did her memory suddenly appear today?

If only he could have seen more of that memorable day long ago. He would have been pleased with what she did at 3:30. Even his 5th grade self would have laughed. The bell rang, all the boys and girls left, and she straightened the desks and chairs while the sound of the school emptied out. After one last look, she shut the door behind her. The empty hall echoed with her unsteady shuffle.

Her pale-yellow car waited in the lot. There was only one other taken spot, a blue utility van, probably the custodian. Otherwise, no one. The rest of the teachers got out fast. The buses had pulled away too. She carried a purse and a big shoulder bag. She wasn't in any rush. She would stop by the Shop N Save on her way home, get some groceries, and make dinner for her grandfather. Magnus Magnusson was 108. Every night he wanted a bowl of string beans. He would be waiting for her in his easy chair, calm as a tortoise.

She opened the door and tossed her bag on the seat. As she sat behind the wheel, she caught sight of herself in the rearview mirror. She bared her steely teeth. "Turn to page forty-two," she said. Mrs. Magnusson got their attention, that was for sure. If she could affect even one of those fifth graders, she thought, it would be worth it. Years from now, thanks to her, they might do something to make the world better. She shook her head and one of those eyes in her glasses darted to the right and stuck. That was too much.

Mrs. Magnusson could only exist for so long. She took off her wig and held it scrunched. Her phony teeth popped out on her palm and she couldn't be quiet anymore—she threw back her head and hooted with laughter. Her disguise was gone, she was a perfectly ordinary looking girl. It was still funny to her, she fooled everyone. She held the dashboard with her other hand and shook.

Caspar's 5th grade self would have loved seeing that. Some things never change.

Caspar crossed the street. The rain had stopped. Sunshine was filling breaks in the clouds. He couldn't stop thinking about Mrs. Magnusson. Believe it or not, on his way home he stopped at the 7-Eleven's telephone booth. He found her name and address in the pulpy thick book bound to the wall.

1917 Maple Street. It wasn't far, just down the street from his house. How strange is that?

It was right in front of him now. Any second he expected to see a rainbow in the sky.

SEA WITCH

She didn't live in a lighthouse, that would only happen in a fairytale, with her black silhouette on a catwalk, luring ships to the rocky shore. No, she lived on the beach, just up from the hightide mark, inside a tangle of driftwood. We found her house on our way home from school.

Sarah found it. I would've walked right past it. It was that well disguised.

Sarah was new to school and I was being her friend. We left our bikes at the edge of the sand and walked towards the sea. You could look a mile each way, left and right. I was watching a seagull ahead of me, wondering if we could catch it and make it ours when Sarah said, "Look!" in that sort of whispery voice you keep for pirates or ghosts.

First, let me make sure you see this the way I do. This isn't a beach in Hawaii. Most days are like this: low gray sky, raindrops fine as powder, choppy cold water, the shapes of islands bursting darkest green. Close to the surf, your footsteps crunch. The ocean must be full of small round stones it pushes ashore. They are pretty as Easter eggs, but if you bring them home, they lose their color. The beach has logs washed up like whales. Some of them could be telephone poles. They are tossed on the sand and stones like those pick-up-stick toys. Sometimes people drag them and fit them together like Lincoln Logs to make simple shelters you can lie in. I know that's what kids from the high school do. I knew that's what Sarah was looking at, but to me it's no big deal. Still, it was new to her, and she wanted to explore and if you want to be someone's friend you do what they like to do.

I like following imagination and I can jump right into games, but I could tell this was no ordinary fort. It looked like a crab buried mostly underground, waiting the way they do for prey or for you to go away. Oh Sarah, why'd you have to find that place and why'd we have to go inside?

Growing up here you wear plaid and a parka, sweaters and boots and I saw the yellow rubber soles of hers as she crawled. You've got to believe me, it really did look like the face of a crab and she got in through its mouth. In a moment, she was looking out the eye, one of the uncovered windows she could see me from. "Come on!" she said. "Wait til you see this place!"

I couldn't be a fraidy cat, even if my feelings told me otherwise, besides my grandmother says we have angels that look out for us, especially when we're kids. Sometimes they're working overtime. The sand slid me down. It was a tight squeeze through that mouth, the logs were sawn rough as teeth.

Sarah laughed as I squirmed my entrance and found myself crawling onto a planed pinewood floor. There was nothing clumsy about the construction, this wasn't clapped together by teenagers dragging bits and pieces across the beach. I stood up next to Sarah and looked around. Whoever made it must not have been much taller than us. Just inches above, smooth branches held each other like arms linked overhead. Seaweed was hanging in strands. Candles made jumpy, orange light, a fireplace readied with a neat pile of tinder. It was warm and dry and made me sleepy.

"This is the kitchen," Sarah said.

"This is someone's house," I told her.

"I know, I love it, I want to live here." She chattered on excitedly about how The Sea Witch was lonely. Something was missing, we both knew it. My new friend wanted to be with her, but not me.

"I think we should go," I said. I didn't know she was so reckless, I guess when you're new you do things nobody else would do. I watched her try a door. It opened and she walked into another room. Past her, I could see more candlelight and wooden walls carved to a bony shine.

She was out of sight, I heard her talking in that room, she wasn't scared. She didn't see the way the hanging kelp and seaweeds began to move with no current or wind. That's when I called her name for the last time. She sounded a mile away, still happy, still wandering around. I turned my head to the fireplace where the cooking pot began to rattle and whine. I jumped when the door to the other room slammed.

The kitchen was twisting like a kaleidoscope, crooked dizzy colors. I ran across the tipped funhouse floor to that shut door. There was no doorknob, no latch or hinges, it was all part of the knuckled wall. The pine floorboards gnashed beneath my feet. The room was alive with snaps and the shrill metallic squeal. I tripped on a branch as I ran to where we dropped in, that crab mouth we had to wriggle through. The wall popped out to greet me, spiny limbs clacked outward like ribs, a cage big enough to trap me in. The windows were gone, no view of the sea, that windowsill with shells and stones was slatted over, the candles were whickering, batting like moths. A floorboard swatted at me. Two more worked together to grab me. I scrambled away towards the fireplace, the shrieking pot big enough to hold a crumpled child, the chimney, the only way out.

It would have been a strange sight for anyone on the beach

that day to see a girl climb from an upright hollow log, to see her pull herself free and fall onto the sand, kicking and clawing across the empty dune.

Sarah was gone. I showed the police the spot where we left our bikes. You could still see the tire treads wetted in the sand and our footprints leading to the shore. I couldn't say what happened though. I said we went to the water, I said I looked away and when I turned around, she was gone. They had a couple boats offshore, looking for a body.

I knew they wouldn't find her that way. It wasn't a story I could tell anyone. For a long time, the sound of that cooking pot haunted me. I could hear it in the wind coming off the sea. I had to keep my window shut, I had to keep the radio on all night long. I was scared to hear the wind, and I was scared to hear the voice of the new girl in the static, or hidden in a song.

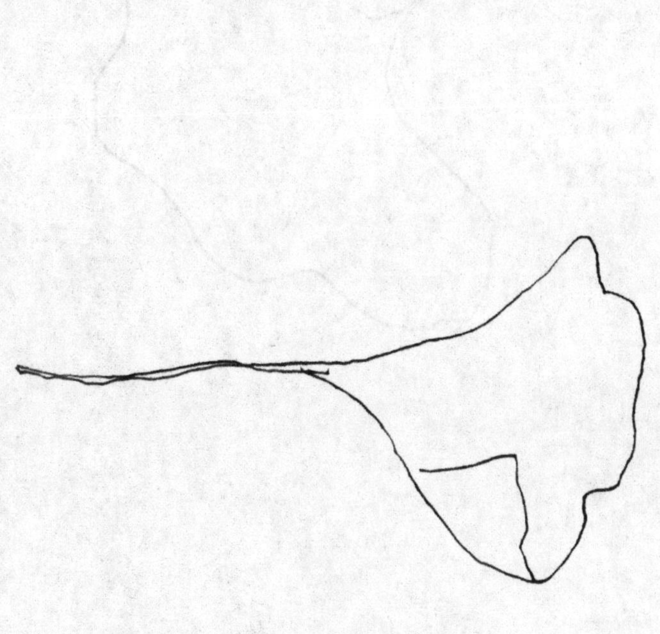

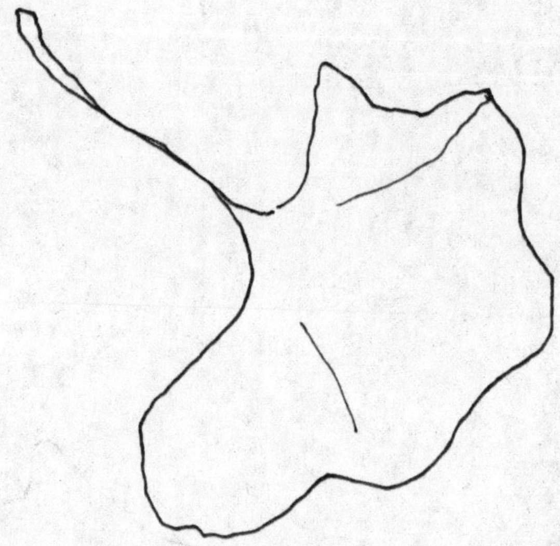

MURDER BY 78

A train rolled into town and stopped and there was a great deal of commotion as they unhooked her personal car and switched it to a sidetrack. A crow landed on the roof of the brick station and watched. It didn't take long before others were appearing. The word spread.

People were excited to see the cursive writing painted on the red siding, *Shelby Wills*. She was a celebrity, star of television's *Murder Conductor*. What was she doing in their little town? She went all around America and nobody every figured out that things were fine before she showed up.

She was wearing her long green coat and her prop hat and she looked just like she was being filmed. Uphill from the tracks, she walked along Central Avenue and turned on Holly Street. She was aware a couple girls followed her from a distance and she waved to a man slumped on a bench. He garbled something to her and she tipped her hat.

Sinbad's Antiques is usually pretty busy and this day was no different. The gloomy clouds helped. What else was there for people to do? The store was cheery, bright, with music from a record player. The people walked along the aisles, laughing, pointing, picking things up. When Shelby Wills walked in, she was the million dollar find in the middle of the room. She heard her name whispered in stereo. Not even the tremolo of the steel guitar could chime over the murmur. Shelby was used to it. She examined the teacups on a wooden shelf.

"Oh, Mrs. Wills, we're such fans of yours here." It didn't take the cashier long to introduce herself and her store.

"Oh," Shelby clucked, as she eyed the woman's delicate porcelain neck.

"If you have a minute, I'd love to show you something. We actually have a whole display devoted to you."

"Do you now?" Shelby followed along, slowing a second past the Japanese sword. When she got there, it was just as she expected. Her merchandise covered a table and the wall behind it. Lunchboxes, cups, replicas of her familiar hat and coat, and a collection of her books. "It's very nice, dear." She offered to sign the poster and some 8x10s. It was the least she could do. She liked the setting, an antique store was always a good place for murder, but this wasn't the scene she was looking for. She saw a stairway leading to the basement level and she had a good feeling about that. While the group of fans were crowded around the display, she made her escape, past a motheaten coat rack and a tall shelf full of Depression era glassware.

A creaking stairway was a good sign. She smiled as the basement appeared before her. It was like descending to a sunken ship graveyard. She steered for the victrola machines. One of those would look picturesque in her railcar. It was a terrible shame that this day and age had forgotten the art of making such things. She would need help getting it back to the tracks. How hard would that be to find a volunteer—the store was crawling with her fans upstairs.

A tabletop was lined with cardboard boxes filled with 78 records. It reminded her of the fish market in Seattle where three people died. She pawed through the names of long ago.

"You a record collector?"

She heard him sidle up to the table. She was hoping to ignore him. But she put on that thin smile and acknowledged him. He smelled like cigarettes and shoe polish. Then she looked back in the box. A 78 was snapped in half. Its jagged edges shined.

"Yeah," he said, "we've got prewar blues, postwar blues, turn of the century opera."

She had seen his type before. There was always another one in the next town.

"To be honest though," he continued, "I don't know how I feel about having you in my section. *Murder Conductor*," he uttered the words like a punchline. "I know about you. I've seen your show. I know anywhere you go, there's murder. See, I got this theory…"

She quickly took note of the empty basement room.

He whispered and leaned closer, "I think anywhere you go, *you* commit the murder."

She froze. That's what a killer usually did. Just before they struck.

"What do you think about that?" he asked.

She picked up the broken 78 half. It was curved and sharp as a dagger.

The BACKWARDS MAN

Millard Delt woke up with his feet on sideways. Of course he couldn't go to work, there was no way he could walk around in an office all day. If only he had a job where he set his own hours, where he could relax and be himself. It was an undertaking just getting to the phone and calling in sick. He left a message and hung up. At least there was no pain. He felt fine, except for the awkwardness of being mobile. Hopefully it wasn't permanent, it would take a lot of getting used to. The best way to move he found was walking like a crab, swinging his arms like claws. Millard managed to totter to the nearest chair and when he collapsed his hands flapped on the armrests. They were turned upside down. What was happening to him?

The phone rang. It was probably work, was his first thought. They were checking up on him. He tried to sit up but couldn't manage it. He felt dizzy. Was his head the next to spin around?

When the phone stopped ringing, there was a beep as the message machine clicked and a husky voice said, "It's me. From last night. You got until noon to get the money to me." That was it. Another click and the room was silent.

He clapped the backs of his hands over his eyes and groaned. He remembered last night, the penny arcade, the lights and crowds and shooting stalls and the card game in the trailer out back. Six poker players around a folding table taking up all the space in the trailer, filling the air with cigarette smoke. Millard lost and kept losing until all his money was gone and he had to sign an IOU before he was allowed out at close to dawn. "You have until noon, or else."

He had no business spending the night at a penny arcade and he paid the price that morning. He wanted to sleep and forget the whole thing, but his metamorphosis wouldn't let him.

He felt his heart jolt as it began to slowly travel to the other side of his body.

"So what if I do turn backwards?" he thought. Big deal. Once I go completely around, I'll be the same as I was before. He looked down his pajama legs and saw his heels. His feet were pointed the other way. He turned on the chair until he was comfortable. With a miserable laugh, he cried, "I couldn't get there by noon if I tried!" What else could he do? He stared at the wallpaper behind the chair and waited patiently for his head to swivel and join the rest of his backwards body.

Only it didn't. The minutes passed. Breathing calm as he could, after half an hour, he seized his head, tried to wrench it around but it wouldn't go. It was cemented on wrong. He wanted to scream. He couldn't look at the wall any longer.

Millard stood and hesitantly took a step. No, it was better to turn around and walk backwards. At least he could see where he was going. He took one, two, three hesitant steps and stopped in the middle of the room. He considered the telephone, trying to hold the receiver up behind his back, while he called for an ambulance. No, he knew they couldn't help, not with medicine. This was the work of a spell, one of those guys at the card table had seen to that. Millard had to pay off his debt or who knows what would happen next.

He made it to the kitchen without falling on his face. He leaned against the counter and reached a backwards arm towards a ceramic jar next to the coffee. Only yesterday he could have grabbed it easily, but now his hands flubbed for it. They didn't even seem like his hands, he felt like a puppeteer. With a loud clack, the jar tipped over and he could see the roll of money. Getting it out was another exercise in contortion. It was a struggle to use arms this way. He unrolled the rubber band and shoved the bills around the countertop until he could manage to count out two hundred dollars. That left him with three dollars to put back in the jar. What was the point? He left them there and folded the debt in his fist and went in the other room.

Getting dressed was an even bigger challenge. He didn't leave the apartment until after eleven o'clock. He wore a heavy overcoat covering a gray suit. A tan wide brimmed fedora shaded his face. He kept his arms loosely held by his sides, his legs moved stiffly—the knees were on wrong—and he hoped nobody looked at his feet. That was the dead giveaway he couldn't hide. Luckily, most people on the sidewalk are intent on their way somewhere, you could be walking a lobster and they wouldn't notice. Millard didn't have far to go, but his rate was slow.

He didn't look right at all. He tried his best to hide it, leaning on a cane as he trudged, going back to where he was the night before. The penny arcade was a different place hit by daylight, the aisles were swept, the shadows were gone, the neon didn't sting the air, and there weren't the swarms of wild-eyed people that clung to the night. He had a little trouble navigating around the Flight to Mars pinball game. On either side of him were more coin operated games, all of them blinking and whining and trying to get his attention like a used robot lot. But the real money was won and lost in the trailer he was shuffling for.

Past the electric chess game, the exit led him outside. He

was retracing his steps. Some pigeons flapped off the cement, over the tangling powerlines. The trailer was just ahead of him. He fumbled for his coat pocket. With difficulty, he felt the cigarettes but when he imagined the contortion necessary to light one, he let his arm drop.

The trailer looked like the tin survivor of a game of Kick the Can. Millard saw his approach blurring on the siding. It's true all gamblers pray. He prayed this payoff would undo the spell. He promised if it did, he would be done with cards. Before he reached the trailer, the dented door opened and there was the evil wizard who did this to him.

"I made it," Millard breathed.

The guy in the doorway scratched his neck. "What's that?" he cupped his ear.

"I said, I made it. I have the money."

"Money? Oh yeah…the money you were supposed to deliver by noon, right?" He tapped the watch on his wrist. "It's past twelve."

"I got here fast as I could. It wasn't easy…Look at me. Look what you did to me?"

"I didn't do that to you. That's what happens to welchers." He got a cigarette and lit it. He made it look easy. "You want one?" he asked Millard.

Millard shuffled forward. He reached for the cigarette, forgetting his arms couldn't reach.

"Come into my palace, we'll talk about your situation." He lit a cigarette for Millard, fed him and stood aside. "Careful on them steps."

Getting up the trailer steps took all Millard's effort. He leaned against the frame and waited to catch his breath. His cigarette bounced as he spoke. It was in danger of falling on the linoleum. "I brought the money. Can't you let bygones?

Please."

"You know, despite being a welch, which you are, you're not a bad guy. Maybe I'll have pity on you." He put a hand on Millard's shoulder. "Let's step into the other room over there, Mill. What say you?"

"Okay…"

The card table was set, waiting for twilight.

"Right in here, Mill." A door creaked open.

Millard froze in the doorway. He had a second to wonder what was going on, then his body snapped and he was falling, landing hard in a pile of straw. He couldn't cushion the fall. He lay on his back with his face buried in the hay. Behind him, the trailer door shut. A lock clicked. He couldn't move for a while, listening to the city for a long time before he groaned. The groan of some animal caged in a zoo. It took all his effort to roll on his shoulder so he could see, so he could read the backwards words of the canvas hanging over the bars: The Backwards Man.

The SONGWRITER

Gail's mother had a Sony tape deck radio on the counter. Whenever she was in the kitchen, it was on. She liked those weepy songs with pianos and heartbroken ballads so sad you wanted to die. She had her favorites. She even wrote one of them. That was after her husband left her, with nothing but little Gail and she turned all her feelings into music. Glen Campbell sang her hit in a movie. She made a little money from it, enough to put a down payment on a house. But any thought of other songs following never materialized. She was strictly a one-hit wonder. Gail Galloway told her friend Ted about her mother's song, but he said he never heard it. Most people hadn't. It was on the chart for a very short while in 1974. Gail took her coat off the hook on the door. The radio was playing The 5th Dimension.

Her mother looked up from her crossword puzzle, "Where are you going?"

"To the movies."

"With someone? Who? A boy?"

"Yes, a boy from school."

"Who is it?"

"You don't know him. Why are you always interfering with my life?"

"What's his name?"

"Mom!" She wrapped a scarf around her neck and buttoned her coat. "I'll be back in a couple hours. We're just going to watch a movie.”

“What movie?”

“Mom!”

“A boy I don’t know, a movie I don’t know—I don’t know anything!” she cried.

“It’s called *Close Encounters of the Third Kind*.”

Her mother’s face pinched, “I don’t like that title.”

“It’s about flying saucers.”

“Oh, Gail! What kind of boy brings a nice girl to a movie like that?”

“His name is Ted. There, now you know everything!”

Gail spun on her heel and blew through the door.

Her mother called down the hallway after her, “Gail! Don’t be gone long! I get worried!”

Gail’s shoes hurried like a bird taking to the air and she practically flew outside.

It was windy, yellow leaves skirted along the curb. She tucked her arms tightly around herself. She didn’t look back. There was a good chance her mother was back there, scuttling after her, it happened before. Once Gail had to hide between a tree and a garage. The sky was gray piled on gray and she felt a raindrop sting her face. Oh no, don’t start raining, she thought, don’t make it worse. The sidewalk slanted up steeply until it reached Aurora Avenue, where she had to catch the bus for a short ride downtown to 4th Avenue. Everyone was going somewhere. She waited and watched and let herself get there.

She saw Ted on the corner. She noticed the way he watched the bus slow, stepping back, and the way he searched the windows looking for her. The Cinerama Theatre was like a big ship waiting to take them away.

She hopped onto the curb, her tennis shoes made a slap, and she waved at him. “Look, there’s already a line!”

"I know, but I was waiting for you."

"You turkey," she gave him a pleasant push. "Come on."

"I like your scarf," Ted said. "It's funny to see you when we're not at school. Like we escaped from prison into the real world."

"Yeah," she said. "And they're looking for us—quick!" she jumped into line. "Let's hide inside this movie theater." It was fun, feeling like she was on the run. They made it to the ticket window without being seen by bounty hunters and she smiled when Ted paid for both of them. That was the sort of guy he was. Her mother didn't know him. He even bought popcorn.

They were halfway through the movie, Teri Garr was taking the kids, when the movie suddenly stopped. The screen went dark and the houselights came on. Everyone groaned. "Excuse me!" a man's voice called from the top of the right aisle. Everyone turned. "We have an unusual situation." A woman was with him.

"Oh no!" Gail seethed. She slumped low in the seat.

"This lady here is looking for her daughter," continued the manager. The woman next to him cried, "Gail!" She held a hand over her eyes and squinted across the rows. "Gail, are you here?" She tottered down the aisle with the manager.

"No, no, no." Gail pulled her coat up over her head. While her mother continued to call her name, the Cinerama crowd was shouting for the movie to return. It was pandemonium. People were standing and jeering the distraught woman, hurling popcorn boxes and candy. Gail bent over low as she scurried into the aisle.

"Where are we going?" Ted asked. He clutched their half full bucket of popcorn.

The manager was trying to restore calm, waving his arms, swiveling and yelling for the projectionist. The lights dimmed again, cheers from the crowd, as Gail pushed through the exit curtains with Ted close behind her. She steamed across the lobby and out the door. No more movie. For all she knew the strange lights in the sky would float forevermore.

Ted had to trot to keep up with her. The popcorn rattled and some of it fell onto the pavement. Down 4th to the end of the block, she turned and hurried. He caught up when she stopped at a store window. He looked back down the street and panted, "I don't see anyone following us."

"She makes me crazy!"

Ted wasn't sure what to do. He stood next to her.

"She thinks she can snoop into everything I do. It's my life!" Gail seethed, "She makes me so mad I don't know what to do."

Ted looked over her shoulder at her reflection.

The display in the record store held her attention. A red guitar leaned on a wooden chair. It was surrounded by albums. A thousand songs. She looked at the guitar and mumbled something. She said it again, louder, and she heard the music behind her as she began to sing.

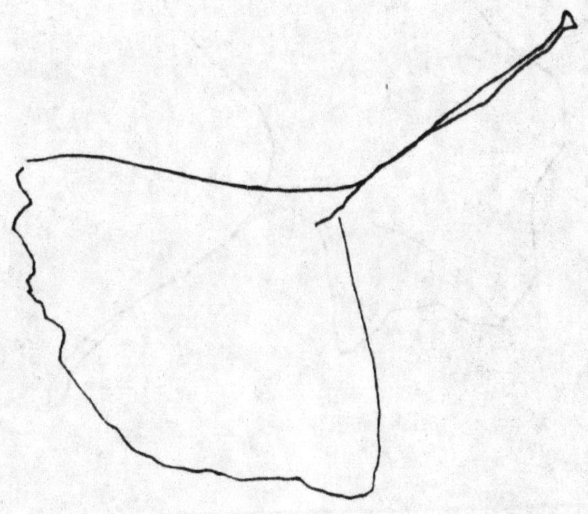

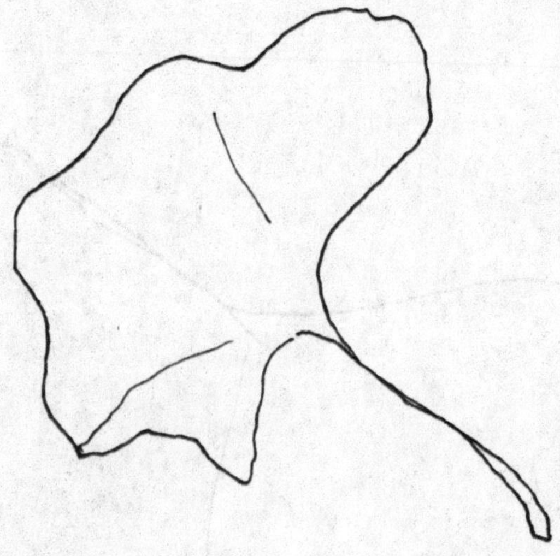

She was excited, why wouldn't she be? It was only her first week and there at Table 5 sat Sylvan Moore. Sandy rushed to the kitchen and told Eileen.

Eileen gave her a look that a going-on eight years waitress has holstered. "Sylvan Moore," she snorted. "Don't get me started." He wasn't the sort to hand out miracles.

"He's my first Hollywood star," Sandy said. "Do you think I could ask for an autograph? No. I better not—they like to be treated like everyone else."

"Yeah, sure." Eileen grabbed three plates and was gone.

Sandy got the glass pot of coffee off the burner and wheeled. She hooked her fingers into two coffee cups and started across the floor to Sylvan Moore.

He was a legend. He had his own late night television talk show since 1962. Her dad used to watch it and he would wake her up if Jonathan Winters was on.

"Would you like some coffee to start with?" she asked, pausing by his table.

He wore sunglasses. His eyes darted off the menu and she almost collapsed.

"I think I'd like some coffee," he said. "Joanne doesn't like coffee, do you?" he asked his companion seated across from him. She barely acknowledged him. Her lacquered nails scratched at the menu.

"Okay, well that's fine," Sandy said, "I'll pour a cup just for you, Mr. Moore."

"Alright, thank you very much." He smiled. White teeth, tan, gold-rimmed sunglasses.

Sandy scooted away. She walked right past another customer holding out an empty cup for her to refill. She spun into the kitchen and went to Eileen. "I just spoke to him!" she gushed.

Eileen wasn't impressed. She was scrubbing a ketchup stain off her apron.

"Oh no!" Sandy clapped her mouth, speaking through her fingers, "I called him Mr. Moore!"

"Order up!" Stanislaw barked.

Eileen shot Sandy a look, "Would you get that for me, hon?"

"Of course." She could see Eileen was busy with that stain. Six plates were lined on the ledge. "Oh gee," Sandy said. She grabbed a tray big enough to carry them all and piled them on. The dishes were heavy but she was walking on the moon. She brought them to Table 2, got them settled without any spills and glanced at Table 5.

The Moores were still reading the menu.

Again, she passed by that same guy with his empty coffee cup.

Sandy wanted a reaction from Eileen. Maybe that was too much to ask for. They had only worked together a few days. Eileen wasn't the type to be starstruck. She cultivated a hardness. Eileen and the black leather jacket she wore. When she hung it on the hook that morning, she told everyone in the kitchen her latest crusade—how she went to that mansion on Belmont and demanded to know how the rich man in there dared to have so much money when poor people like her were barely making it. She hit him up for money too. Sandy was a little intimidated by that. She couldn't imagine doing that. Eileen veered around her with a fresh coffee pot.

Sandy had a flower on her apron string.

She started another pot of coffee.

Sandy wasn't the best waitress, she had maybe half her heart in it half of the time. Meeting Sylvan Moore was magic. She remembered that day for the rest of her life. Fifty years later she opened a faded manilla envelope and set it on her kitchen table. It contained the tip that Sylvan Moore left her. It was hard to believe how time had flown along.

Half a century passed when Sandy gave that envelope to her daughter, who chose to give it to her daughter, telling her, "Your grandma wanted you to have this. She thought it might be worth something."

The envelope was softened by time. Sandy's daughter tipped it and a round flat object fell out. Her daughter saw silver and thought it was a coin, maybe.

The girl knew her mother wouldn't show her right away. First she had to hear the story of, "When your grandma was a waitress, she met Sylvan Moore…"

Sandy's granddaughter was starting out on her own. She was 18. She could use the money. So she brought the heirloom to the pawnshop on Railroad Avenue. An odd assortment filled the window, cluttered together like the parts of an engine that was trying to run again.

She brought the envelope to the counter and said hello to the man sitting there.

"I have something," she told him. She put the envelope on the counter.

The man in the squeaking chair grunted. "What do you have?"

She shook it out onto her palm. A button sized coat pin.

"Sylvan Moore used to be a big star," she said.

The pawnbroker spun it around in his fingers. "Hmm." He turned on his squeaky chair and reached for the thick price guide on the shelf.

"My grandmother met him," she told him. "She was a waitress. He didn't leave her money for a tip. He left her this instead."

The man repeated the red words on the white pin, "I met Sylvan Moore," and he chuckled.

"Is it worth something?" she asked.

"Mmhmm," he answered and looked up from the book closed in place on his hand.

"How much?" she said.

"Twenty-one cents," he answered.

Even after all these years, when he was nothing but a memory, he was the same old cheapskate Sylvan Moore.

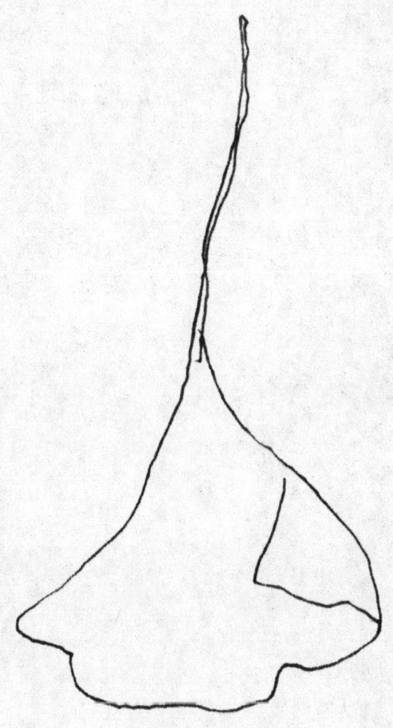

AFTERWORD

Let's pretend that you finished reading this book and are wanting to know more about the stories. Well, I'm glad you asked!

The Next Ichabod Crane. Hah! Working in an office while the day whittles away, I'm often reminded of that poor title character. Like Bartleby the Scrivener, he's one of those classic American archetypes and I'm right in there with them, reports and deadlines, ugh. I nearly fell for a repeat of history, but I decided not to let Ichabod run into that Headless Horseman. After all, he's got enough on his plate.

Cupid Shoots Kid with an Arrow. One of my favorite movies is *The Lady Eve.* It got me through some rough times watching it over and over. I love that moment in the film when Henry Fonda is waiting for Barbara Stanwyck to show up, leaning on the ship railing, and kids are playing somewhere nearby and he's so happy just to know she's on the way.

Alameda Shopper's Gazette. All we had to do was stand in front of the post office handing out flyers, but people started to complain, then someone came from inside and told us to leave or they would call the police. So much for that job. So I went to a café and applied for a dishwashing job and they told me to come by tomorrow for an interview but it was just too much. I didn't want to do that again. When you move somewhere new, you expect the world to change with you.

Animals of the Moon. I originally wrote this story a long time ago when I discovered Raymond Carver and I don't know if you can tell, but this moonlit night owes a lot to him.

Calling Heaven. There are still a couple phonebooths I know of in town, though they're quickly vanishing. Of course they are given magical properties, at least by me, but who knows who uses them now.

How the Civil War Does Linger. For the longest time I kept writing this scene in my notebooks: a parked car with a guy behind the wheel, dressed in a civil war uniform. I finally decided to see where it would go.

The Friendly Sort. Every summer on 32nd Street, a white short-bus from the prison shows up. A crew comes out and they move up the sidewalk, pulling weeds and gleaning garbage from the edge of the road. But I guess this story really began when a friend told me about the time he saw a robber come out of a bank, into the same alley as him, and they looked at each other for just a second.

Mrs. Magnusson. I owe JGenius for telling me of her. I still go by her house, hoping to see her, but she's elusive as the creature in Loch Ness. I take note of the little things I see. Just this last week, walking the dog after work, I noticed she has a hummingbird feeder that glows in the dark.

Sea Witch. On nearby San Juan Island, there's a long beach where logs are washed up and over time they've made a jumble of driftwood along the shore. When we were kids we used to try our hand at making houses out of them. We weren't the only ones. You could always find one that took your imagination a little further.

Murder by 78. In my earlier novel *Island Air*, I introduced Shelby Wills. She is based on the television star, Vera Stanhope. We have trains running through our town and that same antique store, with a slightly different name.

The Backwards Man. A classic nightmare. Sorry, but I get them all the time. They wake me up at 3 AM and I have to deal with them. The best way is to turn them into stories.

The Songwriter. Back in 5th grade, I met my best friend Mel in homeroom. He was reading a book called *Squawk.* His mother has a starring role here, as she really was. And we did see that movie back in 1977, while I was eating Hot Tamales from a paper box.

I Met Sylvan Moore. This story happened thanks to my friend Aaron. Last summer, he told me about a girl he knew in California who was a waitress for Orville Redenbacher, the famous popcorn magnate. I was so shocked and inspired I turned him into a familiar character from my books and he was no different in handing out a tip.

MRS. MAGNUSSON & FRIENDS

Written during October and November 2021

cut from a wet blackboard

Page from *Heaven Crayon* (2020)

Books by Good Deed Rain

Saint Lemonade, Allen Frost, 2014. Two novels illustrated by the author in the manner of the old Big Little Books.

Playground, Allen Frost, 2014. Poems collected from seven years of chapbooks.

Roosevelt, Allen Frost, 2015. A Pacific Northwest novel set in July, 1942, when a boy and a girl search for a missing elephant. Illustrated throughout by Fred Sodt.

5 Novels, Allen Frost, 2015. Novels written over five years, featuring circus giants, clockwork animals, detectives and time travelers.

The Sylvan Moore Show, Allen Frost, 2015. A short story omnibus of 193 stories written over 30 years.

Town in a Cloud, Allen Frost, 2015. A three part book of poetry, written during the Bellingham rainy seasons of fall, winter, and spring.

A Flutter of Birds Passing Through Heaven: A Tribute to Robert Sund, 2016. Edited by Allen Frost and Paul Piper. The story of a legendary Ish River poet & artist.

At the Edge of America, Allen Frost, 2016. Two novels in one book blend time travel in a mythical poetic America.

Lake Erie Submarine, Allen Frost, 2016. A two week vacation in Ohio inspired these poems, illustrated by the author.

and Light, Paul Piper, 2016. Poetry written over three years. Illustrated with watercolors by Penny Piper.

The Book of Ticks, Allen Frost, 2017. A giant collection of 8 mysterious adventures featuring Phil Ticks. Illustrated throughout by Aaron Gunderson.

I Can Only Imagine, Allen Frost, 2017. Five adventures of love and heartbreak dreamed in an imaginary world. Cover & color illustrations by Annabelle Barrett.

The Orphanage of Abandoned Teenagers, Allen Frost, 2017. A fictional guide for teens and their parents. Illustrated by the author.

In the Valley of Mystic Light: An Oral History of the Skagit Valley Arts Scene, 2017. A comprehensive illustrated tribute. Edited by Claire Swedberg & Rita Hupy.

Different Planet, Allen Frost, 2017. Four science fiction adventures: reincarnation, robots, talking animals, outer space and clones. Cover & illustrations by Laura Vasyutynska.

Go with the Flow: A Tribute to Clyde Sanborn, 2018. Edited by Allen Frost. The life and art of a timeless river poet. In beautiful living color!

Homeless Sutra, Allen Frost, 2018. Four stories: Sylvan Moore, a flying monk, a water salesman, and a guardian rabbit.

The Lake Walker, Allen Frost 2018. A little novel set in black and white like one of those old European movies about death and life.

A Hundred Dreams Ago, Allen Frost, 2018. A winter book of poetry and prose. Illustrated by Aaron Gunderson.

Almost Animals, Allen Frost, 2018. A collection of linked stories, thinking about what makes us animals.

The Robotic Age, Allen Frost, 2018. A vaudeville magician and his faithful robot track down ghosts. Illustrated throughout by Aaron Gunderson.

Kennedy, Allen Frost, 2018. This sequel to *Roosevelt* is a coming-of-age fable set during two weeks in 1962 in a mythical Kennedyland. Illustrated throughout by Fred Sodt.

Fable, Allen Frost, 2018. There's something going on in this country and I can best relate it in fable: the parable of the rabbits, a bedtime story, and the diary of our trip to Ohio.

Elbows & Knees: Essays & Plays, Allen Frost, 2018. A thrilling collection of writing about some of my favorite subjects, from B-movies to Brautigan.

The Last Paper Stars, Allen Frost 2019. A trip back in time to the 20 year old mind of Frankenstein, and two other worlds of the future.

Walt Amherst is Awake, Allen Frost, 2019. The dreamlife of an office worker. Illustrated throughout by Aaron Gunderson.

When You Smile You Let in Light, Allen Frost, 2019. An atomic love story written by a 23 year old.

Pinocchio in America, Allen Frost, 2019. After 82 years buried underground, Pinocchio returns to life behind a car repair shop in America.

Taking Her Sides on Immortality, Robert Huff, 2019. The long awaited poetry collection from a local, nationally renowned master of words.

Florida, Allen Frost, 2019. Three days in Florida turned into a book of sunshine inspired stories.

Blue Anthem Wailing, Allen Frost, 2019. My first novel written in college is an apocalyptic, Old Testament race through American shadows while Amelia Earhart flies overhead.

The Welfare Office, Allen Frost, 2019. The animals go in and out of the office, leaving these stories as footprints.

Island Air, Allen Frost, 2019. A detective novel featuring haiku, a lost library book and streetsongs.

Imaginary Someone, Allen Frost, 2020. A fictional memoir featuring 45 years of inspirations and obstacles in the life of a writer.

Violet of the Silent Movies, Allen Frost, 2020. A collection of starry-eyed short story poems, illustrated by the author.

The Tin Can Telephone, Allen Frost, 2020. A childhood memory novel set in 1975 Seattle, illustrated by author like a coloring book.

Heaven Crayon, Allen Frost, 2020. How the author's first book *Ohio Trio* would look if printed as a Big Little Book. Illustrated by the author.

Old Salt, Allen Frost, 2020. Authors of a fake novel get chased by tigers. Illustrations by the author.

A Field of Cabbages, Allen Frost, 2020. The sequel to *The Robotic Age* finds our heroes in a race against time to save Sunny Jim's ghost. Illustrated by Aaron Gunderson.

River Road, Allen Frost, 2020. A paperboy delivers the news to a ghost town. Illustrated by the author.

The Puttering Marvel, Allen Frost, 2021. Eleven short stories with illustrations by the author.

Something Bright, Allen Frost, 2021. 106 short story poems walking with you from winter into spring. Illustrated by the author.

The Trillium Witch, Allen Frost, 2021. A detective novel about witches in the Pacific Northwest rain. Illustrated by the author.

Cosmonaut, Allen Frost, 2021. Yuri Gagarin stars in this novel that follows his rocket landing in an American town. Midnight jazz, folk music, mystery and sorcery. Illustrated by the author.

Thriftstore Madonna, Allen Frost, 2021. 124 summer story poems. Illustrated by the author.

Half a Giraffe, Allen Frost, 2021. A magical novel about a counterfeiter and his unusual, beloved pet. Illustrated by the author.

Lexington Brown & The Pond Projector, Allen Frost, 2022. An underwater invention takes three friends through time. Illustrated by Aaron Gunderson.

The Robert Huck Museum, Allen Frost, 2022. The artist's life story told in photographs, woodcuts, paintings, prints and drawings.

Mrs. Magnusson & Friends, Allen Frost, 2022. A collection of 13 stories featuring mystery and magic and ginkgo leaves.